New Horizon Christian Church Library

MW01097981

DATE DUE

M McG   1954
McGuire, Andy.
Rainy day games : Fun with the Animals of
Noah's Ark

DEMCO

Rainy Day Games

Written and Illustrated by
Andy McGuire

M
McG

1954

For my son, Charlie, owner of the greatest laugh on record.

RAINY DAY GAMES

Copyright © 2008 by Andy McGuire

Published by Harvest House Publishers
Eugene, OR 97402
www.harvesthousepublishers.com

ISBN-13: 978-0-7369-2371-2
ISBN-10: 0-7369-2371-3

TWISTER® & © 2007 Hasbro, Inc. Used with permission.

Artwork © Andy McGuire and published in association with the Books & Such Literary Agency, 52 Mission Circle,
Suite 122, PMB 170, Santa Rosa, CA 95409-5370, www.booksandsuch.biz.

Design and production by Franke Design and Illustration, Minneapolis, Minnesota

All rights reserved. No part of this publication may be reproduced, stored in a retrieval system, or transmitted
in any form or by any means—electronic, mechanical, digital, photocopy, recording, or any other—
except for brief quotations in printed reviews, without the prior permission of the publisher.

Printed in Hong Kong

08 09 10 11 12 13 14 15 /NG/ 10 9 8 7 6 5 4 3 2 1

Before we get started...

A flood was coming. God told Noah he needed to build a big boat for his family and
two of every kind of animal. Noah probably guessed it wouldn't be easy. First of all,
boats are tough to build. Also, people would laugh at him. And, of course, everybody
knows llamas and rhinos hate to sail. But maybe worst of all, can you imagine
staying indoors for 40 rainy days in a row? What would they do to pass the time?

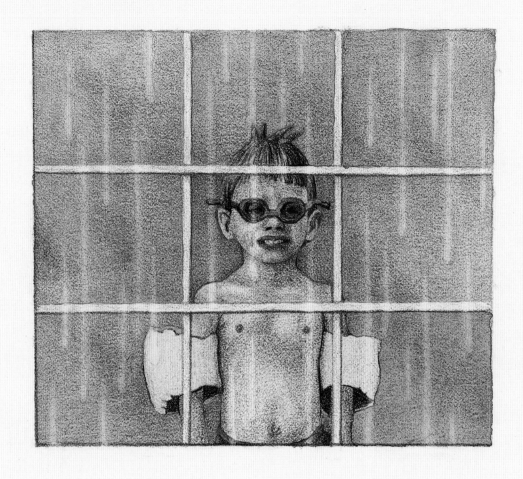

W hen it's been raining night and day,
And you don't know what games to play,

Pretend that Noah's ark floats by,
And watch the games that they would try.

Hide-and-seek can be a treat.
Chameleons can be tough to beat.

To tease your brain on stormy days,
You have to try a zebra maze.

Untangle a flamingo knot.

A diagram will help a lot.

It's fun to play ring-tosseros.

At least it's fun for *most* of us!

A game of Ping-Pong never fails.
Beavers choose to use their tails.

Double Dutch takes lots of practice.
Poison dart frogs jump the fastest!

Jacks with yaks can be a blast.

A sloth-race winner gets there last.

Blindmole's bluff is good for laughs.

New Horizon Christian Church Library
14038 E 350 N Road
P.O. Box 147
Heyworth, IL 61745

And Twister's fun with two giraffes.

A croc-o-dial will make you smile.

And soccer's fun...

For a little while.

Watch a wallaby jump a hurdle.

Play turtle-tac-toe.

Or tic-tac-turtle.

See what sticks to a porcupine.
Grapes and cherries stick just fine.

Try tiddlywinks with a clever mink.

Or, if you're brave, play "Name That Stink."

A cheetah's back has lots of spots,
Where you can play connect-the-dots.

What a ride it is to slide

Down the side of an elephant's hide.

Try playing something
from our list.

And think of other games
we missed.

Or just sit back as clouds go by,
Until God's rainbow paints the sky.

New Horizon Christian Church Library
14038 E 350 N Road
P.O. Box 147
Heyworth, IL 61745